JAY BUBBLEBEE

The Bee Who Started It All

Look for the second book of the
JAY BUBBLEBEE series
by Kyle Dixon III December 2014.
Enter Kyle's name at www.amazon.com
to search for his book.

Send Kyle a message at:
https://www.facebook.com/KyleDixonIII

JAY BUBBLEBEE

The Bee Who Started It All

by KYLE DIXON III

Illustrated by Donell Hagan

To all Hungry Bees that are ready to soar without wings.
If you start now, you can become greatness!

CONTENTS

1

WHO IS IT?

Buzz, Buzz, Buzz! Every minute the bee-shaped hand buzzed around the clock a hair on Mr. Bubblebee's head would stand up. He fidgeted at the kitchen table. Jay set the iced sweet-nectar-filled pitcher down. Julie followed with a warm loaf of bee bread.

"Dinner looks delicious kids," Mr. Bubblebee said in a low voice.

"Thanks Dad," Jay said, as he sat.

Julie smiled at her father.

The family laughed and ate.

Knock, Knock, Knock.

"I'll get it," Jay said as he stuffed the extra helping of bee bread in his mouth. He opened the door.

"Hello, is your father home?" Mr. Head Horn asked.

Jay's mouth was still packed. He grinned and nodded.

"Excuse me," Mr. Bubblebee said as he gently nudged Jay to the side. "Hello, Mr. Head Horn."

Something about Mr. Head Horn's sharp horn and big eyes made Jay's stomach turn.

"Is this your son?" Mr. Head Horn asked with a smirk as he pointed to Jay.

"Yes, this is my oldest son, Jay," Mr. Bubblebee said as he opened the door wide. "And that's my daughter Julie."

Julie waved.

"How's the shoe business coming along?" Mr. Head Horn asked as he scratched his pointy chin.

"It *was* a disaster!" Mr. Bubblebee replied. "That was until *The Bee Hive No Flying* decision was passed yesterday. All insects must now walk inside town Bee Hive. No more bees flying into one another."

"That was a crazy ruling," Mr. Head Horn responded, grinding his teeth.

"We finally feel normal living here," Mr. Bubblebee said without blinking.

Jay smiled.

"Normal?" Mr. Head Horn crossed his arms tightly. "Your family chose bubbles instead of wings. You will never be able to fly out of this town. You will never fit in here."

Mr. Bubblebee boldly stood tall.

Mr. Head Horn crept closer and towered over them. "I stopped by to remind you the money is due Sunday."

"Yes, I know," Mr. Bubblebee replied, shuffling from foot to foot. A bubble the size of a baseball drifted from his back.

Pop!

The bubble burst in Jay's face.

Mr. Bubblebee walked onto the porch. He closed the door behind him.

"Well, since I am such a nice hornet," Mr. Head Horn said, "I know you're having a hard time coping with your wife's passing. I also understand running a business while raising kids must be difficult. So I decided to let you have the money."

Jay listened behind the door. He gazed at the hardwood floor. His eyes filled.

"Mr. Head Horn, I can't thank you enough!" Mr. Bubblebee shouted. "I was so worried. I didn't know how I would get the money by Sunday. This is great news."

"I want your *house*," Mr. Head Horn said.

Jay gulped behind the door.

"I will trade the money for your home!" Mr. Head Horn said.

"My house *isn't* for sale!" Mr. Bubblebee screamed. "The only way you will get this house is if I can't pay you, and I will pay you in full by Sunday."

"Have it your way!" Mr. Head Horn stomped off the porch.

Jay hurried to the kitchen.

His father walked inside and closed the door. Mr. Bubblebee slowly sat down on the couch.

"What am I going to do?" he said as he bowed his head and covered his face with his hands.

2

JUST A KID

Mr. Bubblebee wiped the sweat from his wrinkled forehead and buttoned his furry vest.

"Hey Daddy," Julie said as she cheerfully washed the dishes. "The kitchen is almost clean."

Jay stopped sweeping. He looked up at his father. Then he began sweeping again.

"Thank you, Jay and Julie," Mr. Bubblebee said. "I'll finish cleaning the kitchen. Both of you can get ready for bed. I have a lot of work to do tonight in the Shoe Den."

Mr. Bubblebee lifted Julie off of the stool. Her sleeves were soaked.

"Dad, can *I* help?" Jay asked.

"Jay, you're just a kid," Mr. Bubblebee chuckled. "It's past both of your bedtimes. Goodnight."

Jay's blood boiled as he and Julie walked to their separate bedrooms.

"Goodnight Jay," Julie said in a baby's voice. Her snaggle-toothed smile grew wider.

Jay slammed his door. He kicked the blue sneaker that lay on the floor. He stood in front of the mirror. His hazel eyes turned brown. *"Jay, you can't do this because you're a kid,"* he said, mimicking his father's voice. *"Jay, you can't do that because you have bubbles instead of wings.* I'm tired of being treated like a toddler. There is no limit to what I can do!"

Jay plopped down on his bed. He laid back and fell asleep.

Tap, Bang, Tap! The noise awoke him.

Jay put on his slippers and snuck downstairs. He tiptoed through the kitchen, then hid behind the wall.

Tap, Tap, Tap!

His father hit the machine. Jay had been spying on his father for a couple of months. He had secretly learned how to make shoes by watching him.

Something was caught in the machine. A small piece of brown fabric.

The Den was full of bubbles. His dad paced around the machine.

Jay's heart beat faster. This was his chance to prove to his dad that he was more than just a kid.

Jay slid from behind the wall. "Hey, Dad." Jay pulled the jammed cloth out of the machine. "Here's why the machine wouldn't work." Jay handed the cloth to Mr. Bubblebee.

Mr. Bubblebee put his taped safety glasses on. He turned on the switch.

Rrrrrrr!

Startled, Mr. Bubblebee froze. "Jay, you are a genius!" he declared.

Jay's cheeks reddened. He had finally proved that he could do something!

"Wait a second!" Mr. Bubblebee yelled. "I thought I told you to go to bed?"

3

TRYING TO HELP!

"I'm sorry," Jay said. "I was only trying to help!"

"I know, son," Mr. Bubblebee said.

"Dad, can I ask you a question?"

"I'm listening."

"Have you ever wished for wings instead of bubbles?"

"Of course I have. Sometimes I still do. Growing up in Bubble Hive as a kid was amazing. All insects had bubbles. Wings were unheard of. Once jobs were invented everyone had to make a choice. Create your own destiny by keeping your bubbles or trade your bubbles for wings to work. My father chose the bubbles."

"Wow, Dad! I never knew. May I ask another question?"

"Of course."

"Why do you owe Mr. Head Horn money?"

"I had a feeling you were listening behind the door!" Mr. Bubblebee's eyes grew wider than two bowling balls. He turned away from Jay and then pointed to the shoe machine. "I wanted to finally be my own boss! I had built up enough courage to follow my dream by quitting my job. Mr. Head Horn was not happy that I was leaving, but he explained that he understood."

Jay sucked at his big front teeth.

"He offered to lend me the money to buy a shoe machine," Mr. Bubblebee said. "I accepted the money. He gave me sixty days to pay it back. If I wasn't able to pay within that time given, he would then own our home."

"Well, that's not going to happen!" Mr. Bubblebee rubbed a handful of sweet-scented honey lotion over his blistered fingers. "The Spring Festival is in a couple of days. It's the perfect opportunity to raise funds to save our home."

Mr. Bubblebee and Jay went to work. They created twenty pairs of black sneakers.

"Jay, please hand me the red dye on the desk."

Jay grabbed it. He ran back to give it to his father.

Wham!

Jay slipped. His hand hit the floor. The red dye flew in the air and splattered.

"Jay, look what you've done!" Mr. Bubblebee's brows pulled together tightly.

The red dye spilled all over the black sneakers. They were ruined.

"I didn't mean it!" Jay's lips quivered as the guilt crunched in his belly.

"Just go to bed, Jay! Maybe when you are older I will give you another try. But, right now, you're just a kid. Goodnight."

Jay stormed out of the Shoe Den.

"Maybe kids can't do anything right," Jay mumbled as he marched up the steps. He walked into his room, closed the door, and lay on his bed.

Boom, Bang, Boom!

Jay quickly sat up. He thought he heard tussling.

Boom, Bam, Boom!

Jay inched toward the door.

The banging got louder and louder.

"Ah!"

A faint scream? He moved closer to the door in horror. He grabbed the knob. Slowly he turned it.

4

OPEN IT!

Jay opened the door. The noise suddenly stopped.

Something was wrong.

Huh woo! Jay took a deep breath.

"Go to bed," Jay said in his father's voice. Dad must have jammed the machine again. "Oh well, this time he can't blame me."

Jay yawned, turned around, and hopped into his bed. He closed his eyes. Then he fell fast asleep.

The morning sun beat down on Jay's face. He stretched his arms. Feeling good, he got dressed and then started to brush his messy hair.

"Jay!" Julie screamed, as she opened Jay's door.

Startled, he dropped his brush on the floor. "Julie, I told you to knock before coming into my room!"

"Daddy is missing!" she shouted.

Jay ran to his father's room. Julie followed. Jay searched around. The bed looked as if it had not been slept in.

"Did you check downstairs?" Jay asked.

"I checked everywhere!" Julie grabbed her antennas. She quickly tied them around her forehead to make a headband.

Jay ran down the steps. Julie stumbled behind him.

"How did the door get wide open?" Jay asked.

"It wasn't me," Julie said with a shrug.

Jay looked outside the open door. No insects were in sight. The sun even began to hide. Jay shut the door and locked it.

"Dad!" Jay yelled. He rushed through the kitchen and into the Shoe Den. Julie trailed behind him.

Jay's eye's widened. His father's desk was turned over, chair legs were broken, and torn fabric was all over the floor.

"Look!" Julie pointed. She was looking at the exact spot where Jay had spilled the dye on the black shoes and the floor. Written in the red dye was the word *help*!

Jay trembled.

"Jay, you okay?"

Jay stood in silence.

"Jay!" Julie yelled as she shook him.

Jay snapped out of the daze. His gut feeling was correct. Something had been wrong when he heard all those noises the night before.

"We have to find other clues," Jay said. "I will search this side, and you search the other."

Julie searched her side of the Den. She picked up the fabrics. She threw them into her father's fabric chest.

The door, from top to bottom, was almost torn off the hinges. Jay pushed the door backward. A small object fell to the floor. Jay picked up the white, hard object—it had a point on one end. "What's this?" Jay said as he poked at it in his hand.

Knock, Knock, Knock!

"That must be Dad!" Julie ran out of the Shoe Den.

Jay followed. He looked at the object again. "It's the tip of a horn!" Jay gasped. "Julie, wait! Don't open the door!"

Bang, Bang, Bang!

Jay ran to Julie. She had already opened the door.

"Well, hello, little girl!" the sheriff said.

Jay yanked his sister behind him. He opened the door wider.

Standing on the porch was Mr. Head Horn and the sheriff. The sheriff held a yellow envelope. "Is your dad home?" The sheriff stood up straight.

"Sheriff, our dad is missing!" Julie said as she peeked from behind. "We can't find him!"

The sheriff's eyes protruded. His belly grew bigger and popped open his shirt. He held the shirt together.

Mr. Head Horn laughed.

Mr. Head Horn looked somewhat different today. His dark hair was slicked back, and it made his horn appear whiter. The horn was chipped. Jay squeezed the broken piece he held in his hand. Bubbles began to drift from his flimsy yellow jacket.

"My sister meant that my dad left early this morning," Jay said. "He's been working nonstop."

Julie nudged him.

The sheriff tilted his egg-shaped head.

"When will he be back?" Mr. Head Horn asked.

He'll be back shortly!" Jay said.

Jay went to close the door.

The sheriff's stubby hand stopped it. "Please give this envelope to your father." He handed Jay the envelope. He used his other hand to secure his shirt.

Jay grabbed the envelope and then slowly closed the door. Mr. Head Horn and the sheriff walked off the porch.

Jay and Julie gazed at the big yellow envelope. They glanced at each other.

"We have to open it!" Jay glided his finger across the edge. "It's the only way we'll know how much Dad owes Mr. Head Horn."

5

GREAT IDEA

Rip!

Jay opened the envelope and pulled out the long sheet of paper.

"What does it say?" Julie asked as she yanked his arm.

Jay read aloud the typewritten message on the paper: *I, Mr. Bubblebee, agree to repay Mr. Head Horn five hundred sugar dollars within sixty days. If unable to pay, Mr. Head Horn will be the new owner of the Bubblebee residence.*

"Oh no, Julie," Jay dropped the paper on the floor. "What are we going to do? We won't have any place to go, and Dad is still missing." A large amount of bubbles rushed from his back.

Julie stood back. "Is everything going to be okay?" Julie asked, lifting her little beady eyes. "Is it, Jay?"

Jay kneeled down. He plucked her pointy nose.

Julie giggled.

"I promise," Jay said, crossing his sweaty fingers. "We won't lose another parent. We will save our house. That is what *bee go-getters* do!"

"We need a job!" Julie shouted.

"That's great idea, Julie. Well, let's go find one!"

They walked out and locked the door. Jay looked up at the gloomy sky.

"There!" Julie pointed.

A group of bees worked outside.

"Excuse me," Jay whispered.

The bees continued to work. He glanced at Julie.

"Louder," Julie demanded.

"Can anyone hear me?" Jay yelled. "We need a job!"

All the bees stopped working. They stared at Jay and Julie as if their heads were on backward.

"Yes, I can hear you!" Mrs. Queen Bee shouted as she walked out of the huge building. She slammed the door. She swung a piece of her golden hair away from her face. "Who told you bees to stop working? Get back to work!"

The bees began working again.

"What can I help you kids with today?" Mrs. Queen Bee smiled, showing the smeared purple lipstick on her front tooth.

"Well, I'm not actually a kid anymore," Jay said, with a bashful smile. "I am ten years old!"

Mrs. Queen Bee rolled her big brown eyes. "I don't hire kids," Mrs. Queen Bee said, blowing her breath. She impatiently stomped her heels.

Jay and Julie both put their heads down. They turned and walked away.

"Wait!" Mrs. Queen Bee yelled. "I don't usually do this. But when you both turn sixteen, I will hire you!"

"Sixteen is a million years from now!" Julie said, boldly lifting her hands. "I'm only six."

"We need a job now!" Jay said.

"Well, I can't hire you now," Mrs. Queen Bee said. "You're too young and have no experience. However, Mr. Nosey hires kids to collect honey and pays them. His building is right around the corner. Tell him Mrs. Queen Bee sent you!"

"Thanks, Mrs. Queen Bee," Jay said. "Let's go, Julie!"

Jay and Julie approached the building. It was shaped like a nose. A group of kids stood in line in front of the building. A skinny bee with a big nose held a clipboard.

Jay and Julie slowly walked toward them.

"Steven, Billy, Hamilton, Kyle," Mr. Nosey called as he crept down the line. He stopped. "Just a moment, kids, I smell two visitors."

Jay and Julie sniffed their underarms.

"It's not me!" Julie squinted toward Jay.

Mr. Nosey turned with his head held high. His chin bulged forward.

"Hello, Mr. Nosey!" Jay said.

"No, it's pronounced *No-say*!" Mr. Nosey's eyes turned red.

Julie hid behind Jay.

"I'm sorry, Mr. No-say," Jay said. "My sister and I are looking for a job."

Mr. Nosey laughed. "How can I give you a job? Neither of you have wings!

"This is true," Mr. Nosey said, brushing back the last hair on his balding head. "I hire kids with wings that don't mind taking low wages!"

Mr. Nosey spun Jay around. He examined him. Bubbles floated from his back. "The young bees I hire work outside of the hive. Bees with bubbles will never be accepted outside Town Bee Hive. I am sorry. There is nothing I can do for you here! Flier, Nicky, Chase." Mr. Nosey called. He walked away.

The time without light drew near. A cold shudder trickled down Jay's spine.

"I don't think we'll get the money," Julie whimpered.

"Let's go home, Julie. I don't think we'll get the money today. Dad should be home by now. We can take the short cut to get there faster."

Julie folded her little hands.

Jay and Julie turned down into the alley. It was very dark, narrow, and filled with barrels. They shivered as they walked.

"Jay, I am starting to get scared!"

They walked faster. They were almost to the end of the spooky alley. A patch of light exposed the remaining trail. Jay heard a familiar voice. Goose bumps broke out on their arms.

6

IT'S OVER

Jay and Julie peeked around the corner. Mr. Head Horn stood talking to a Young Hornet with a red jacket. On the jacket were the initials P.S.

"Tomorrow we will have a new Problem Starters Headquarters!" Mr. Head Horn said, chuckling.

"Where will it be?" the Young Hornet asked as he brushed off his sparkling jacket.

"There was a Shoemaker that used to work for me," Mr. Head Horn said. "He lived in the house right there." He pointed to Jay and Julie's house. "He wanted to start his own business. I tried to talk him out of it. He wouldn't listen, so I had to come up with a plan. I didn't want my other workers to think they could start their own business, too!"

The Young Hornet shook his head.

"I knew I needed to get rid of him fast!" Mr. Head Horn rubbed his hands together. "So I offered to give him the money to buy a shoe machine. I had him sign a paper that he would pay me back in sixty days. If he couldn't do it, I'd be able to take his home and his dream business."

Jay's goose bumps disappeared. His antennas stood at attention.

"I thought it would be impossible for him to get the money!" Mr. Head Horn said. "That's until Mrs. Queen Bee passed the "no flying in Bee Hive" ruling, and I began seeing a lot of insects with shoes on. I knew then I had to get rid of him, and that's what *I* did."

Jay antlers dropped. He glanced at his little sister.

Julie's eyes closed tight and her mouth opened wide.

"Julie, don't!" Jay murmured.

"Aah Choo!"

The Young Hornet turned. "Someone's there!"

"Run, Julie!" Jay shouted.

Jay and Julie ran. The Young Hornet gained on them.

Julie's short legs could not keep up. "Ah!" Julie screamed as she tripped over her long fluffy tutu dress.

The Young Hornet closed in on her.

Jay sprinted back. He grabbed her hand and pulled her up. "Run home, Julie!" Jay stayed behind to let his sister get away.

Julie took off. She stopped and looked back with tears in her eyes.

The Young Hornet snatched Jay's jacket sleeves.

"Go!" Jay yelled to Julie, and saliva sprinkled everywhere.

"You are coming with *me*!" The Young Hornet pulled Jay back into the spooky alley.

"What were you two doing here?" Mr. Head Horn asked. His huge muscled arms twitched.

"We were on our way home!" Jay tried to pull away from the Young Hornet. He couldn't. The Young Hornet was strong. "Where's my dad?"

"First, tell me what you heard?" Mr. Head Horn pried.

"I know you set my dad up!" Jay yelled.

"Well, it's too bad you won't have the chance to tell anyone!" Mr. Head Horn said. He opened a barrel. It was filled with green, bubbling-hot bug poisoning. "Your dad is gone. I'm doing Bee Hive a favor by getting rid of your family. What's a bee without wings? *Absolutely nothing!*"

"I'm not sure," Jay said as he tilted his head. "I guess it's the same as a hornet with no stinger that hides behind toxic poison!"

Mr. Head Horn slowly glanced back. "Throw him in!" Mr. Head Horn demanded.

The Young Hornet forced Jay forward. They moved closer to the barrel. Jay's jacket began to melt.

Jay's heart pounded louder than a beating drum. "*No!*" Jay shouted.

7

GET AWAY!

Mr. Head Horn stroked his chin.

"No way am I going in there!" Jay kicked the barrel with all his might. The barrel tipped over.

Splash!

The boiling poison spilled onto the ground. It bubbled and ate through the ground. The awful stench reeked of rotten eggs and spoiled meat.

Mr. Head Horn climbed up the brick wall.

"Wow!" The Young Hornet said.

Jay pushed the Young Hornet back with his arm. The Young Hornet stumbled and fell backward. Jay darted out of the alley.

Huuh, huuh, huuh! Jay breathed loudly. His heart pounded harder with each step. The bubbles from Jay's back came out quickly as he ran.

Mr. Head Horn easily popped the bubbles with his horn. His long legs moved faster than a windmill.

Jay hurried up the porch steps.

"Julie, let me in!" Jay banged on the door.

Julie looked out the window. She saw Jay and unlocked the door.

"Hurry!" Jay shouted.

The door opened. Jay dashed inside the house. He closed the door and locked it.

"What are we going to do?" Julie asked.

Jay ran to the window. Mr. Head Horn stood there, staring at him. Mr. Head Horn turned and walked away.

Jay closed the curtain. "Julie, Mr. Head Horn has Dad! And I don't think we'll get the money either. It's time for us to give up!"

"Don't ever say that, Jay!" Julie wiped her tear-stained face. "I know what we can do. We can sell shoes."

"Impossible." Jay shook his head. "We're kids, with limits. Remember? No one believes kids can do anything until they are grown!"

"I still believe! Julie shouted. "I am going to try!" Julie went into the Shoe Den.

Jay slumped onto the living room couch. He picked at the holes in his torn jeans.

"How do you turn on this thing?" Julie yelled.

Jay lifted up his head. "Here I come!" he yelled as he ran to the Shoe Den.

8

ANYTHING IS POSSIBLE

"Don't touch anything," Jay said as he entered the room.

Julie stood still; she was holding a pair of black shoes with red dye on them.

Jay snickered. "We can't do anything with those shoes."

"We can sell them."

"Julie, no insect will want those shoes. They are ruined. We'll have to make our own. A shoe that is different from any other."

"Other insects always call us that word," Julie said with a frown.

"What word?" Jay asked.

"Different!"

Jay stood in silence. Julie was right. They had always been called different. All the other flying insects had wings. They were free to roam outside the Bee Hive, but the Bubblebees were not.

"What if we made the other insects look like us?" Jay asked with a big smile. "How about Bubble Sneakers? We can call them Jay Bubbles."

"Jay, our bubbles only last for one day." Julie's dainty brows and nose scrunched together. "No insect will buy shoes for only one day."

"Well, let's see what Dad has in here."

They searched the whole room.

Julie opened the fabric chest. She moved the fabric, dyes, and other materials around. "I give up!" She put her hands on her waist. "I don't know what I should be looking for. I'm going to sleep. Have fun creating your Jay Bubbles." Julie slammed the trunk closed and walked out of the den.

Jay sat on the trunk. "I'm not going to give up." He ran around the room. The room filled with bubbles. Jay sat and stared. He quickly grabbed a pencil and paper. "A bubble is round and clear. That's it! I need a clear material to make the sneakers!"

Jay now knew what he was searching for. He opened the trunk. At the bottom was twenty-five clear-plastic long sheets. And twenty-five soles for the bottoms of the shoes.

"Found it!" Jay yelled.

Jay drew the frame of the shoe. He used the plastic sheets to cut twenty-five pairs of shoe patterns. Once he molded the frames, he put the frames, plastic, and soles all together. All twenty-five pairs were ready to be permanently bonded together.

"Here goes nothing," Jay said. He took a deep breath. He flipped on the machine switch.

The belt began to move. Jay placed a pair of sneakers on the slide. The belt moved the sneakers forward under the covering.

"Here they come!" Jay ran to the other side. He anxiously waited for the sneakers to come out.

"What happened?" The melted shoes came from underneath the covering. Jay continued to run four more pairs through the shoe machine. They all melted.

"Maybe kids do have limits!" Jay said with a low voice.

He glanced over to the fabric trunk. A big poster board hung above it. The poster had instructions on how to use the shoe machine.

"Today must be my lucky day!"

The instructional poster explained three different settings. High, medium, and low—depending on the fabric or material.

"Aha!" Jay walked back to the shoe machine. The current setting was on high. "So that's why the shoes were melting!" He turned the setting to low. He put all twenty shoes on the belt.

Each Bubble Sneaker came out perfect!

"I did it!" His heart danced. He could do anything!

Jay turned off the machine and cleaned up. He then inspected all twenty pairs of sneakers individually on the long shoe belt. He was so amazed. He fell peacefully asleep after staring at the Bubble Sneakers most of the night.

Unexpectedly, a loud familiar voice screamed, *"Wake up!"*

9

THE BIG DAY

"Dad?" Jay rubbed the sleep out of his eyes.

"Wake up, silly!" Julie shook him. "You must be dreaming!"

"What time is it, Julie?"

"It's nine in the morning." Julie opened the curtains. The sun rays glistened through the window.

"Nine o' *clock*?" Jay jumped off the floor.

"Wow!" Julie yelled, pointing at the freshly made Bubble Sneakers. "Jay, these are great!"

Jay smiled even bigger. "We have to go! The Spring Festival is today! We need to get there early to get a table to sell the shoes."

"But Jay, how will we carry all of the sneakers?"

Jay walked into the kitchen. He snatched off the big grassy-designed tablecloth and ran back into the Shoe Den. "Problem solved!" He laid the tablecloth on the floor.

They placed the sneakers on it. Jay held one end. Julie held the other end. Together they walked three blocks to reach the festival.

"Look, Jay!" Julie began to twirl around. "We're here!"

The Festival was filled with flies, mosquitos, honeybees, and bumblebees. The insects were waggling to the music, talking to one another, buying products, and eating.

Jay and Julie grabbed the last open table. They placed all twenty sneakers neatly on the table.
"Julie, here's the plan," Jay whispered. "Each pair of sneakers will be sold for twenty-five sugar dollars. If we sell all twenty pairs at this amount, we will make

five hundred sugar dollars. That's enough money to save our home, so we can focus on finding Dad!"

Julie tied her messy hair with her antennas. They smiled as insects passed their table.

Two hours had gone by and they hadn't sold any shoes.

"Jay, I don't think we're going to make it," Julie said softly.

"Watch the table, I will be back." Jay walked around the festival. Everyone was selling items except for them. Insects stood in line to buy shoes. They just weren't at their Bubble Sneakers table.

His sneakers were better than all the others at the fair. So why weren't they selling anything? The others had colorful signs made of cardboard.

"Where will I get a sign?" Jay hurried back to their table. "Maybe it's time for us to give up."

Jay walked past a trashcan filled with empty boxes. Jay grabbed a box and ran back to their table. "Look what I have!" he said with a smile.

Julie's smile faded.

"What are you doing, Julie?"

"I'm packing up!" She grabbed the last shoe off of the table. She placed it on the tablecloth.

"Julie, we can't give up!" He removed the shoes from the tablecloth and placed each one back on the table.

At the table next to him, Mr. Nosey was painting faces.

Jay ran over to him. "Hello, Mr. Nosey!"

Mr. Nosey snarled.

"I mean, Mr. No-say!"

"I thought that was you over there," Mr. Nosey said. "What are you selling?"

"Bubble Sneakers!" Jay stuck his scrawny chest out. He pointed to their table. "May I please borrow some of your paint and yarn?"

"Well, since I wasn't able to give you a job…"

Jay frowned.

"And since you are persistent, I will gladly give you three finger paints and a spool of yarn!"

Jay grabbed the yellow, blue, and red finger paints. He also picked one spool of gold yarn. "Thank you for everything," Jay said with a smile. He walked back to the table and grabbed the box.

10

TIME IS UP!

Jay pushed out the sides of the box. It was now a big cardboard. Jay wrote: Bubble Sneakers, $25 Sugar Bucks.

"Julie, I need your help!" He separated twenty pieces of yarn. "Place the long piece of yarn around each pair of shoes."

Jay ran around the table. Bubbles flew everywhere. A large number of insects walked toward the Bubble Sneakers table.

"Bubble Sneakers, twenty-five sugar bucks for your Bubble Sneakers!" Jay yelled.

Bubbles with sneakers inside them floated in the air. Jay and Julie held onto them with the yarn.

"What are those?" an Older Bee asked as she gawked at the sneakers in the air.

"They're Bubble Sneakers!" Jay said.

"How're they different from other shoes?" the Older Bee asked, tugging her wing on straight.

Jay handed the Older Bee a bubble with yarn attached. The Older Bee popped it. She put the clear sneakers on her feet.

"These feel great!" The Older Bee danced around in them. "Every step feels like I'm floating!"

The insect crowd laughed.

"I will take two pair!" the Older Bee said.

"The sneakers are made for kids and grownups," Jay said. "No longer does an insect have to remove their shoes when going out of the Bee Hive. With Bubble Sneakers, no one will know the difference.

"I want a pair."

"Me, too!"

Within minutes, Jay and Julie had sold all of their Bubble Sneakers. They made their five hundred sugar dollars. All the insects at the fair had wanted a pair. They were sold out.

"We have to go," Jay said to the crowd. "But we promise to have more soon!"

Jay and Julie quickly cleaned their area.

They ran, headed for home to make more Bubble Shoes.

"Wait!" someone yelled.

Jay stopped and turned back. Mrs. Queen Bee was walking toward him. This time she had green lipstick smeared on her teeth.

"Hey, Mrs. Queen Bee," Jay said.

"I wanted to let you know that you impressed me today," Mrs. Queen Bee said. "If you still want to work for me, I am willing to hire my first kid!"

Jay thought about it. "No thanks, Mrs. Queen Bee. I no longer need a job." Jay waved her goodbye.

Jay and Julie sprinted all the way home. Someone stood at their front door.

The sheriff and Mr. Head Horn had begun to put a big lock on the door.

"Wait!" Jay screamed.

"Time is up," Mr. Head Horn said. "Your father is not here to pay the money." He smiled and winked. "I now own the property."

Jay handed the sheriff the money. He counted it.

"There's all the money my dad owed to start his business," Jay said.

"All the money is here," the sheriff said. He handed Mr. Head Horn the money.

Mr. Head Horn counted it. "This is impossible— coming from kids!" He threw the money to the ground.

"Maybe it was impossible when you were a kid, but not for us," Jay said.

The sheriff took the big lock off of the door. He lifted his hat to all, and he left.

Mr. Head Horn's eyes looked like daggers, ready to aim at Jay. "This isn't over!"

"You're right," Jay said. "This *isn't* over. Not until we get our dad back home. We will not lose another parent."

Jay and Julie walked away from Mr. Head Horn. A breeze whisked the money down the road. Each step they took up onto the porch, the bigger their smiles grew.

Kids *could* do anything if they pressed Bee-yond their limits!

"Now to find Dad!"

To be continued...

ABOUT THE AUTHOR

Kyle Dixon III is the twelve-year-old author of the Jay Bubblebee Series. He was inspired to write his first book after witnessing his single parent mother quit her full time job to spend more time with him. Since then his mother has become a successful entrepreneur and would forever spark the courage and confidence in Kyle to not wait until he's older to live his dreams of owning his own business.